Ten-Gallon Bart

By Susan Stevens Crummel   Illustrated by Dorothy Donohue

Marshall Cavendish Children

en-Gallon Bart was sheriff of Dog City. Had been for ten years—that's seventy in dog years. Bart was brave, courageous, and bold. Why, when Miss Kitty got stuck in a tree, it was Bart to the rescue! When Buffalo Gal got her hoof tangled in a fence, it was Bart to the rescue! He'd done his job and done it well. Dog City was the most peaceful town in the West.

But Bart was tired of being brave, courageous, and bold. He wanted to sleep until noon, howl at the moon, and go fishing anytime he wanted. So he decided to step down. Hang up his star. Retire. And today was his last day.

Ten-Gallon Bart started
this day just like any other.
He opened the morning paper.
His breath stopped.

County Fair News

Sheriff to Retire

After 10 years (70 in
dog years), our brave
courageous, and bold
Sheriff, Ten-Gallon
Bart, is stepping down.
A big woof for
Sheriff Bart!

d for best fried
Fair last

The headlines read,

Billy the Kid on the Loose!
Headed for Dog City on the Noon Train

Bart looked at the clock. 10:30. An hour and a half till noon. His legs shook. His paws trembled. His jowls quivered. "Th-th-this can't be! Not on my last day as sheriff!"

Billy the Kid was the roughest, toughest, gruffest goat in the country. He ate anything and everything in his way—soap and rope, saddles and paddles, socks and clocks. You name it, he ate it. And now he was headed for Dog City. On the noon train. And the only one who could stop him was Ten-Gallon Bart!

~ The Daily Muzzle ~
BILLY THE KID ON THE LOOSE!
HEADED FOR DOG CITY ON THE NOON TRAIN

The roughest, toughest, leanest, meanest goat in the country is headed for our beloved town. He just ate purdy near all of the three towns near Gopher Hill. Everyone needs to take cover. Hide your belongings. Hide your ____'s no tellin' what's fixin' BILLY THE K____ outta Dog City

Miss Kitty rushed in. "Bart! Bart! Have you heard the news? Billy the Kid is headin' our way! You gotta do something! He'll munch our flowers! He'll chomp our trees! He'll—"

"Whoa, Miss Kitty! Don't get your fur in a fluff."

"But, Sheriff—he's dangerous! He'll gobble up this whole town! You're the only one who can stop him. You're brave, courageous, and—"

"And OLD!" Bart interrupted. "I'm old, and I'm tired of being sheriff. Remember? I'm hangin' up my star!"

"Please stay! We need you. You won't be alone," cried Miss Kitty. "We'll be there. We'll do our part. We're behind you, Sheriff Bart!"

Ten-Gallon Bart went looking for his deputies, Wild
Bill Hiccup and Wyatt Burp. When he walked past the
chicken coop, he heard familiar noises.

HIC, BURP!

"Bill, Wyatt—you hidin' in there?" asked Bart.
"Nobody in here but a couple of roosters,
COCK-A-DOODLE–DOO-OO!"

HIC, BURP!

"Hogwash! A couple of chickens is
more like it!" yelled Bart. "Billy the
Kid'll be here soon. For one last
day, I'm the sheriff, and
YOU'RE my deputies. Come
outta there and get back to
work or I'll be fixin'
bacon for breakfast!"

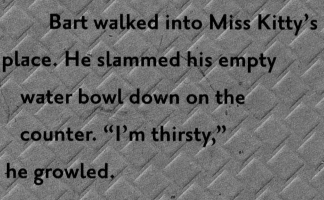

Bart walked into Miss Kitty's place. He slammed his empty water bowl down on the counter. "I'm thirsty," he growled.

Miss Dixie filled his bowl fast. "Mighty brave of you to stay on the job, Sheriff. I mean, with Billy the Kid comin' and all. Most dogs woulda hightailed it outta here."

Bart sighed. "A dog's gotta do what a dog's gotta do."

Buffalo Gal brought him some dog biscuits. "We'll be there. We'll do our part. We're behind you, Sheriff Bart!"

Everyone gathered on Main Street.
Bart called roll.

"Miss Kitty?" MEOW!

"Pixie and Dixie?" CLUCK, CLUCK!

"Buffalo Gal?" M-O-O!

"Wyatt?" BURP!

"Wild Bill?" HICCUP!

Bart stood tall in his ten-gallon hat.

"Thanks for helpin' out. Now, let's meet that train."

The townsfolk cheered. "We'll be there. We'll do our part. We're behind you, Sheriff Bart!"

Miss Kitty
Pixie
Dixie
Buffalo
Wyatt
Wild

TOOT
TO-O-O-OT!

The train screeched to a halt. A figure slowly appeared.

It was Billy the Kid. His eyes swept the crowd. He licked his lips. Then he yelled at the top of his lungs,

"I'm BAA-AA-AA-AA-D!!"

Everyone in the town ran for cover. Everyone except Ten-Gallon Bart.